Kenneth Grahame  ·ction

Kenneth Grahame was born on 8th March 1

At age 5 his mother succumbed to puerperal ... ..ing problem, now sent his 4 children to live with their grandmother a... ...oknam, Berkshire. Here the children lived in large open grounds next to the river. T... ...xperiences would in later years, be retold in his writing through a myriad of characters.

Grahame loved being a pupil at St Edward's School, Oxford and wanted to enroll at the university there but his guardian demurred on account of the cost.

Instead, a banking career was chosen for him, starting in 1879 at the Bank of England, where he rose steadily to the rank of its Secretary until retiring, with a pension, in 1908 due to ill health.

Alongside his commercial career Grahame had written and published various stories and essays in several periodicals. Some were anthologized as 'Pagan Papers' in 1893, and two years later 'The Golden Age' and later still 'Dream Days' and its masterpiece 'The Reluctant Dragon' became part of many home libraries. His ability to view life through the lens of a young and curious child was superb, enabling the reader to easily identify with the character.

Grahame married Elspeth Thomson in 1899 and they had one child; Alastair, born semi-blind and plagued by health problems. In a heart-rending tragedy he would later take his own life whilst attending Oxford University in 1920.

In 1908 Grahame reworked many of the bedtime stories he had fashioned for his son into the enduring favourite; 'The Wind in the Willows', describing the heart-warming adventures of Mr Toad and his friends.

Kenneth Grahame died in Pangbourne, Berkshire, on 6th July 1932.

Index of Contents

A Saga of the Seas

It happened one day that some ladies came to call, who were not at all the sort I was used to. They suffered from a grievance, so far as I could gather, and the burden of their plaint was Man—Men in general and Man in particular. (Though the words were but spoken, I could clearly discern the capital M in their acid utterance.)

Of course I was not present officially, so to speak. Down below, in my sub-world of chair-legs and hearthrugs and the undersides of sofas, I was working out my own floor-problems, while they babbled on far above my head, considering me as but a chair-leg, or even something lower in the scale. Yet I was listening hard all the time, with that respectful consideration one gives to all grown-up people's remarks, so long as one knows no better.

It seemed a serious indictment enough, as they rolled it out. In tact, considerateness, and right appreciation, as well as in taste and aesthetic sensibilities—we failed at every point, we breeched and bearded prentice-jobs of Nature; and I began to feel like collapsing on the carpet from sheer spiritual anaemia. But when one of them, with a swing of her skirt, prostrated a whole regiment of my brave tin soldiers, and never apologized nor even offered her aid toward revivifying the battle-line, I could not help feeling that in tactfulness and consideration for others she was still a little to seek. And I said as much, with some directness of language.

That was the end of me, from a society point of view. Rudeness to visitors was the unpardonable sin, and in two seconds I had my marching orders, and was sullenly wending my way to the St. Helena of the nursery. As I climbed the stair, my thoughts reverted somehow to a game we had been playing that very morning. It was the good old game of Rafts,—a game that will be played till all the oceans are dry and all the trees in the world are felled—and after. And we were all crowded together on the precarious little platform, and Selina occupied every bit as much room as I did, and Charlotte's legs didn't dangle over any more than Harold's. The pitiless sun overhead beat on us all with tropic impartiality, and the hungry sharks, whose fins scored the limitless Pacific stretching out on every side, were impelled by an appetite that made no exceptions as to sex. When we shared the ultimate biscuit and circulated the last water-keg, the girls got an absolute fourth apiece, and neither more nor less; and the only partiality shown was entirely in favour of Charlotte, who was allowed to perceive and to hail the saviour-sail on the horizon. And this was only because it was her turn to do so, not because she happened to be this or that. Surely, the rules of the raft were the rules of life, and in what, then, did these visitor-ladies' grievance consist?

Puzzled and a little sulky, I pushed open the door of the deserted nursery, where the raft that had rocked beneath so many hopes and fears still occupied the ocean-floor. To the dull eye, that merely tarries upon the outsides of things, it might have appeared unromantic and even unraftlike, consisting only as it did of a round sponge-bath on a bald deal towel-horse placed flat on the floor. Even to myself much of the recent raft-glamour seemed to have departed as I half-mechanically stepped inside and curled myself up in it for a solitary voyage. Once I was in, however, the old magic and mystery returned in full flood, when I discovered that the inequalities of the towel-horse caused the bath to rock, slightly, indeed, but easily and incessantly. A few minutes of this delightful motion, and one was fairly launched. So those women below didn't want us? Well, there were other women, and other places, that did. And this was going to be no scrambling raft-affair, but a full-blooded voyage of the Man, equipped and purposeful, in search of what was his rightful own.

Whither should I shape my course, and what sort of vessel should I charter for the voyage? The shipping of all England was mine to pick from, and the far corners of the globe were my rightful inheritance. A frigate, of course, seemed the natural vehicle for a boy of spirit to set out in. And yet there was something rather "uppish" in commanding a frigate at the very first set-off, and little spread was left for the ambition. Frigates, too, could always be acquired later by sheer adventure; and your real hero generally saved up a square-rigged ship for the final achievement and the rapt return. No, it was a schooner that I was aboard of—a schooner whose masts raked devilishly as the leaping seas hissed along her low black gunwale. Many hairbrained youths started out on a mere cutter; but I was prudent, and besides I had some inkling of the serious affairs that were ahead.

I have said I was already on board; and, indeed, on this occasion I was too hungry for adventure to linger over what would have been a special delight at a period of more leisure—the dangling about the harbour, the choosing your craft, selecting your shipmates, stowing your cargo, and fitting up your private cabin with everything you might want to put your hand on in any emergency whatever. I could not wait for that. Out beyond soundings the big seas were racing westward and calling me, albatrosses hovered motionless, expectant of a comrade, and a thousand islands held each of them a fresh adventure, stored up, hidden away, awaiting production, expressly saved for me. We were humming, close-hauled, down the Channel, spray in the eyes and the shrouds thrilling musically, in much less time than the average man would have taken to transfer his Gladstone bag and his rugs from the train to a sheltered place on the promenade-deck of the tame daily steamer.

So long as we were in pilotage I stuck manfully to the wheel. The undertaking was mine, and with it all its responsibilities, and there was some tricky steering to be done as we sped by headland and bay, ere we breasted the great seas outside and the land fell away behind us. But as soon as the Atlantic had opened out I began to feel that it would be rather nice to take tea by myself in my own cabin, and it therefore became necessary to invent a comrade or two, to take their turn at the wheel.

This was easy enough. A friend or two of my own age, from among the boys I knew; a friend or two from characters in the books I knew; and a friend or two from No-man's-land, where every fellow's a born sailor; and the crew was complete. I addressed them on the poop, divided them into watches, gave instructions I should be summoned on the first sign of pirates, whales, or Frenchmen, and retired below to a well-earned spell of relaxation.

That was the right sort of cabin that I stepped into, shutting the door behind me with a click. Of course, fire-arms were the first thing I looked for, and there they were, sure enough, in their racks, dozens of 'em—double-barrelled guns, and repeating- rifles, and long pistols, and shiny plated revolvers. I rang up the steward and ordered tea, with scones, and jam in its native pots—none of your finicking shallow glass dishes; and, when properly streaked with jam, and blown out with tea, I went through the armoury, clicked the rifles and revolvers, tested the edges of the cutlasses with my thumb, and filled the cartridge- belts chock-full. Everything was there, and of the best quality, just as if I had spent a whole fortnight knocking about Plymouth and ordering things. Clearly, if this cruise came to grief, it would not be for want of equipment.

Just as I was beginning on the lockers and the drawers, the watch reported icebergs on both bows—and, what was more to the point, coveys of Polar bears on the icebergs. I grasped a rifle or two, and hastened on deck. The spectacle was indeed magnificent—it generally is, with icebergs on both bows, and these were exceptionally enormous icebergs. But I hadn't come there to paint Academy pictures, so the captain's gig was in the water and manned almost ere the boatswain's whistle had ceased sounding, and we were pulling hard for the Polar bears—myself and the rifles in the stern-sheets.

I have rarely enjoyed better shooting than I got during that afternoon's tramp over the icebergs. Perhaps I was in specially good form; perhaps the bears "rose" well. Anyhow, the bag was a portentous one. In later days, on reading of the growing scarcity of Polar bears, my conscience has pricked me; but that afternoon I experienced no compunction. Nevertheless, when the huge pile of skins had been hoisted on board, and a stiff grog had been served out to the crew of the captain's gig, I ordered the schooner's head to be set due south. For icebergs were played out, for the moment, and it was getting to be time for something more tropical.

Tropical was a mild expression of what was to come, as was shortly proved. It was about three bells in the next day's forenoon watch when the look-out man first sighted the pirate brigantine. I disliked the looks of her from the first, and, after piping all hands to quarters, had the brass carronade on the foredeck crammed with grape to the muzzle.

This proved a wise precaution. For the flagitious pirate craft, having crept up to us under the colours of the Swiss Republic, a state with which we were just then on the best possible terms, suddenly shook out the skull-and-cross-bones at her masthead, and let fly with round-shot at close quarters, knocking into pieces several of my crew, who could ill be spared. The sight of their disconnected limbs aroused my ire to its utmost height, and I let them have the contents of the brass carronade, with ghastly effect. Next moment the hulls of the two ships were grinding together, the cold steel flashed from its scabbard, and the death-grapple had begun.

In spite of the deadly work of my grape-gorged carronade, our foe still outnumbered us, I reckoned, by three to one. Honour forbade my fixing it at a lower figure—this was the minimum rate at which one dared to do business with pirates. They were stark veterans, too, every man seamed with ancient sabre-cuts, whereas my crew had many of them hardly attained the maturity which is the gift of ten long summers—and the whole thing was so sudden that I had no time to invent a reinforcement of riper years. It was not surprising, therefore, that my dauntless boarding-party, axe in hand and cutlass between teeth, fought their way to the pirates' deck only to be repulsed again and yet again, and that our planks were soon slippery with our own ungrudged and inexhaustible blood. At this critical point in the conflict, the bo'sun, grasping me by the arm, drew my attention to a magnificent British man-of-war, just hove to in the offing, while the signalman, his glass at his eye, reported that she was inquiring whether we wanted any assistance or preferred to go through with the little job ourselves.

This veiled attempt to share our laurels with us, courteously as it was worded, put me on my mettle. Wiping the blood out of my eyes, I ordered the signalman to reply instantly, with the half- dozen or so of flags that he had at his disposal, that much as we appreciated the valour of the regular service, and the delicacy of spirit that animated its commanders, still this was an orthodox case of young gentleman-adventurer versus the unshaved pirate, and Her Majesty's Marine had nothing to do but to form the usual admiring and applauding background. Then, rallying round me the remnant of my faithful crew, I selected a fresh cutlass (I had worn out three already) and plunged once more into the pleasing carnage.

The result was not long doubtful. Indeed, I could not allow it to be, as I was already getting somewhat bored with the pirate business, and was wanting to get on to something more southern and sensuous. All serious resistance came to an end as soon as I had reached the quarter-deck and cut down the pirate chief—a fine black-bearded fellow in his way, but hardly up to date in his parry-and-thrust business. Those whom our cutlasses had spared were marched out along their own plank, in the approved old fashion; and in tune the scuppers relieved the decks of the blood that made traffic temporarily impossible. And all the time the British-man-of-war admired and applauded in the offing.

As soon as we had got through with the necessary throat-cutting and swabbing-up all hands set to work to discover treasure; and soon the deck shone bravely with ingots and Mexican dollars and church plate.

There were ropes of pearls, too, and big stacks of nougat; and rubies, and gold watches, and Turkish Delight in tubs. But I left these trifles to my crew, and continued the search alone. For by this time I had determined that there should be a Princess on board, carried off to be sold in captivity to the bold bad Moors, and now with beating heart awaiting her rescue by me, the Perseus of her dreams.

I came upon her at last in the big state-cabin in the stern; and she wore a holland pinafore over her Princess-clothes, and she had brown wavy hair, hanging down her back, just like—well, never mind, she had brown wavy hair. When gentle-folk meet, courtesies pass; and I will not weary other people with relating all the compliments and counter-compliments that we exchanged, all in the most approved manner. Occasions like this, when tongues wagged smoothly and speech flowed free, were always especially pleasing to me, who am naturally inclined to be tongue-tied with women. But at last ceremony was over, and we sat on the table and swung our legs and agreed to be fast friends. And I showed her my latest knife—one-bladed, horn-handled, terrific, hung round my neck with string; and she showed me the chiefest treasures the ship contained, hidden away in a most private and particular locker—a musical box with a glass top that let you see the works, and a railway train with real lines and a real tunnel, and a tin iron-clad that followed a magnet, and was ever so much handier in many respects than the real full-sized thing that still lay and applauded in the offing.

There was high feasting that night in my cabin. We invited the captain of the man-of-war—one could hardly do less, it seemed to me—and the Princess took one end of the table and I took the other, and the captain was very kind and nice, and told us fairy- stories, and asked us both to come and stay with him next Christmas, and promised we should have some hunting, on real ponies. When he left I gave him some ingots and things, and saw him into his boat; and then I went round the ship and addressed the crew in several set speeches, which moved them deeply, and with my own hands loaded up the carronade with grape-shot till it ran over at the mouth. This done, I retired into the cabin with the Princess, and locked the door. And first we started the musical box, taking turns to wind it up; and then we made toffee in the cabin-stove; and then we ran the train round and round the room, and through and through the tunnel; and lastly we swam the tin ironclad in the bath, with the soap-dish for a pirate.

Next morning the air was rich with spices, porpoises rolled and gambolled round the bows, and the South Sea Islands lay full in view (they were the real South Sea Islands, of course—not the badly furnished journeymen-islands that are to be perceived on the map). As for the pirate brigantine and the man-of-war, I don't really know what became of them. They had played their part very well, for the time, but I wasn't going to bother to account for them, so I just let them evaporate quietly. The islands provided plenty of fresh occupation. For here were little bays of silvery sand, dotted with land-crabs; groves of palm-trees wherein monkeys frisked and pelted each other with cocoanuts; and caves, and sites for stockades, and hidden treasures significantly indicated by skulls, in riotous plenty; while birds and beasts of every colour and all latitudes made pleasing noises which excited the sporting instinct.

The islands lay conveniently close together, which necessitated careful steering as we threaded the devious and intricate channels that separated them. Of course no one else could be trusted at the wheel, so it is not surprising that for some time I quite forgot that there was such a thing as a Princess on board. This is too much the masculine way, whenever there's any real business doing. However, I remembered her as soon as the anchor was dropped, and I went below and consoled her, and we had breakfast together, and she was allowed to "pour out," which quite made up for everything. When breakfast was over we ordered out the captain's gig, and rowed all about the islands, and paddled, and explored, and hunted bisons and beetles and butterflies, and found everything we wanted. And I gave her pink shells and tortoises and great milky pearls and little green lizards; and she gave me guinea pigs, and coral to make into, waistcoat-buttons; and tame sea-otters, and a real pirate's powder-horn. It was a prolific day and a long-lasting one, and weary were we with all our hunting and our getting and our gathering, when at last we clambered into the captain's gig and rowed back to a late tea.

The following day my conscience rose up and accused me. This was not what I had come out to do. These triflings with pearls and parrakeets, these al fresco luncheons off yams and bananas—there was no "making of history" about them. I resolved that without further dallying I would turn to and capture the French frigate, according to the original programme. So we upped anchor with the morning tide, and set all sail for San Salvador.

Of course I had no idea where San Salvador really was. I haven't now, for that matter. But it seemed a right-sounding sort of name for a place that was to have a bay that was to hold a French frigate that was to be cut out; so, as I said, we sailed for San Salvador, and made the bay about eight bells that evening, and saw the top-masts of the frigate over the headland that sheltered her. And forthwith there was summoned a Council of War.

It is a very serious matter, a Council of War. We had not held one hitherto, pirates and truck of that sort not calling for such solemn treatment. But in an affair that might almost be called international, it seemed well to proceed gravely and by regular steps. So we met in my cabin—the Princess, and the bo'sun, and a boy from the real-life lot, and a man from among the book-men, and a fellow from No-man's-land, and myself in the chair. The bo'sun had taken part in so many cuttings-out during his past career that practically he did all the talking, and was the Council of War himself. It was to be an affair of boats, he explained. A boat's-crew would be told off to cut the cables, and two boats'-crews to climb stealthily on board and overpower the sleeping Frenchmen, and two more boats'-crews to haul the doomed vessel out of the bay. This made rather a demand on my limited resources as to crews; but I was prepared to stretch a point in a case like this, and I speedily brought my numbers up to the requisite efficiency.

The night was both moonless and starless—I had arranged all that—when the boats pushed off from the side of our vessel, and made their way toward the ship that, unfortunately for itself, had been singled out by Fate to carry me home in triumph. I was in excellent spirits, and, indeed, as I stepped over the side, a lawless idea crossed my mind, of discovering another Princess on board the frigate—a French one this time; I had heard that that sort was rather nice. But I abandoned the notion at once, recollecting that the heroes of all history had always been noted for their unswerving constancy. The French captain was snug in bed when I clambered in through his cabin window and held a naked cutlass to his throat. Naturally he was surprised and considerably alarmed, till I discharged one of my set speeches at him, pointing out that my men already had his crew under hatchways, that his vessel was even then being towed out of harbour, and that, on his accepting the situation with a good grace, his person and private property would be treated with all the respect due to the representative of a great nation for which I entertained feelings of the profoundest admiration and regard and all that sort of thing. It was a beautiful speech. The Frenchman at once presented me with his parole, in the usual way, and, in a reply of some power and pathos, only begged that I would retire a moment while he put on his trousers. This I gracefully consented to do, and the incident ended.

Two of my boats were sunk by the fire from the forts on the shore, and several brave fellows were severely wounded in the hand-to-hand struggle with the French crew for the possession of the frigate. But the bo'sun's admirable strategy, and my own reckless gallantry in securing the French captain at the outset, had the fortunate result of keeping down the death-rate. It was all for the sake of the Princess that I had arranged so comparatively tame a victory. For myself, I rather liked a fair amount of blood-letting, red-hot shot, and flying splinters. But when you have girls about the place, they have got to be considered to a certain extent.

There was another supper-party that night, in my cabin, as soon as we had got well out to sea; and the French captain, who was the guest of the evening, was in the greatest possible form. We became sworn friends, and exchanged invitations to come and stay at each other's homes, and really it was quite difficult to induce him to take his leave. But at last he and his crew were bundled into their boats; and after I had pressed some pirate bullion upon them—delicately, of course, but in a pleasant manner that admitted of no denial—the gallant fellows quite broke down, and we parted, our bosoms heaving with a full sense of each other's magnanimity and good fellowship.

The next day, which was nearly all taken up with shifting our quarters into the new frigate, so honourably and easily acquired, was a very pleasant one, as everyone who has gone up in the world and moved into a larger house will readily understand. At last I had grim, black guns all along each side, instead of a rotten brass carronade: at last I had a square-rigged ship, with real yards, and a proper quarter-deck. In fact, now that I had soared as high as could be hoped in a single voyage, it seemed about time to go home and cut a dash and show off a bit. The worst of this ocean-theatre was, it held no proper audience. It was hard, of course, to relinquish all the adventures that still lay untouched in these Southern seas. Whaling, for instance, had not yet been entered upon; the joys of exploration, and strange inland cities innocent of the white man, still awaited me; and the book of wrecks and rescues was not yet even opened. But I had achieved a frigate and a Princess, and that was not so bad for a beginning, and more than enough to show off with before those dull unadventurous folk who continued on their mill-horse round at home.

The voyage home was a record one, so far as mere speed was concerned, and all adventures were scornfully left behind, as we rattled along, for other adventurers who had still their laurels to win. Hardly later than the noon of next day we dropped anchor in Plymouth Sound, and heard the intoxicating clamour of bells, the roar of artillery, and the hoarse cheers of an excited populace surging down to the quays, that told us we were being appreciated at something like our true merits. The Lord Mayor was waiting there to receive us, and with him several Admirals of the Fleet, as we walked down the lane of pushing, enthusiastic Devonians, the Princess and I, and our war-worn, weather-beaten, spoil-laden crew. Everybody was very nice about the French frigate, and the pirate booty, and the scars still fresh on our young limbs; yet I think what I liked best of all was, that they all pronounced the Princess to be a duck, and a peerless, brown- haired darling, and a true mate for a hero, and of the right Princess-breed.

The air was thick with invitations and with the smell of civic banquets in a forward stage; but I sternly waved all festivities aside. The coaches-and-four I had ordered immediately on arriving were blocking the whole of the High Street; the champing of bits and the pawing of gravel summoned us to take our seats and be off, to where the real performance awaited us, compared with which all this was but an interlude. I placed the Princess in the most highly gilded coach of the lot, and mounted to my place at her side; and the rest of the crew scrambled on board of the others as best they might. The whips cracked and the crowd scattered and cheered as we broke into a gallop for home. The noisy bells burst into a farewell peal—

Yes, that was undoubtedly the usual bell for school-room tea. And high time too, I thought, as I tumbled out of the bath, which was beginning to feel very hard to the projecting portions of my frame-work. As I trotted downstairs, hungrier even than usual, farewells floated up from the front door, and I heard the departing voices of our angular elderly visitors as they made their way down the walk. Man was still catching it, apparently—Man was getting it hot. And much Man cared! The seas were his, and their islands; he had his frigates for the taking, his pirates and their hoards for an unregarded cutlass-stroke or two; and there were Princesses in plenty waiting for him somewhere—Princesses of the right sort.

Dies Irae

Those memorable days that move in procession, their heads just out of the mist of years long dead—the most of them are full-eyed as the dandelion that from dawn to shade has steeped itself in sunlight. Here and there in their ranks, however, moves a forlorn one who is blind—blind in the sense of the dulled window-pane on which the pelting raindrops have mingled and run down, obscuring sunshine and the circling birds, happy fields, and storied garden; blind with the spatter of a misery uncomprehended, unanalysed, only felt as something corporeal in its buffeting effects.

Martha began it; and yet Martha was not really to blame. Indeed, that was half the trouble of it—no solid person stood full in view, to be blamed and to make atonement. There was only a wretched, impalpable condition to deal with. Breakfast was just over; the sun was summoning us, imperious as a herald with clamour of trumpet; I ran upstairs to her with a broken bootlace in my hand, and there she was, crying in a corner, her head in her apron. Nothing could be got from her but the same dismal succession of sobs that would not have done, that struck and hurt like a physical beating; and meanwhile the sun was getting impatient, and I wanted my bootlace.

Inquiry below stairs revealed the cause. Martha's brother was dead, it seemed—her sailor brother Billy; drowned in one of those strange far-off seas it was our dream to navigate one day. We had known Billy well, and appreciated him. When an approaching visit of Billy to his sister had been announced, we had counted the days to it. When his cheery voice was at last heard in the kitchen and we had descended with shouts, first of all he had to exhibit his tattooed arms, always a subject for fresh delight and envy and awe; then he was called upon for tricks, jugglings, and strange, fearful gymnastics; and lastly came yarns, and more yarns, and yarns till bedtime. There had never been any one like Billy in his own particular sphere; and now he was drowned, they said, and Martha was miserable, and—and I couldn't get a new bootlace. They told me that Billy would never come back any more, and I stared out of the window at the sun which came back, right enough, every day, and their news conveyed nothing whatever to me. Martha's sorrow hit home a little, but only because the actual sight and sound of it gave me a dull, bad sort of pain low down inside—a pain not to be actually located. Moreover, I was still wanting my bootlace.

This was a poor sort of a beginning to a day that, so far as outside conditions went, had promised so well. I rigged up a sort of jurymast of a bootlace with a bit of old string, and wandered off to look up the girls, conscious of a jar and a discordance in the scheme of things. The moment I entered the schoolroom something in the air seemed to tell me that here, too, matters were strained and awry. Selina was staring listlessly out of the window, one foot curled round her leg. When I spoke to her she jerked a shoulder testily, but did not condescend to the civility of a reply. Charlotte, absolutely unoccupied, sprawled in a chair, and there were signs of sniffles about her, even at that early hour. It was but a trifling matter that had caused all this electricity in the atmosphere, and the girls' manner of taking it seemed to me most unreasonable. Within the last few days the time had come round for the despatch of a hamper to Edward at school. Only one hamper a term was permitted him, so its preparation was a sort of blend of revelry and religious ceremony. After the main corpus of the thing had been carefully selected and safely bestowed—the pots of jam, the cake, the sausages, and the apples that filled up corners so nicely—after the last package had been wedged in, the girls had deposited their own private and personal offerings on the top. I forget their precise nature; anyhow, they were nothing of any particular practical use to a boy. But they had involved some contrivance and labour, some skimping of pocket money, and much delightful cloud-building as to the effect on their enraptured recipient. Well, yesterday there had come a terse acknowledgment from Edward, heartily commending the cakes and the jam, stamping the sausages with the seal of Smith major's approval, and finally hinting that, fortified as he now was, nothing more was necessary but a remittance of five shillings in postage stamps to enable him to face the world armed against every buffet of fate. That was all. Never a word or a hint of the personal tributes or of his appreciation of them. To us—to Harold and me, that is—the letter seemed natural and sensible enough. After all, provender was the main thing, and five shillings stood for a complete equipment against the most unexpected turns of luck. The presents were very well in their way—very nice, and so on—but life was a serious matter, and the contest called for cakes and half-crowns to carry it on, not gew-gaws and knitted mittens and the like. The girls, however, in their obstinate way, persisted in taking their own view of the slight. Hence it was that I received my second rebuff of the morning.

Somewhat disheartened, I made my way downstairs and out into the sunlight, where I found Harold playing conspirators by himself on the gravel. He had dug a small hole in the walk and had laid an imaginary train of powder thereto; and, as he sought refuge in the laurels from the inevitable explosion, I heard him murmur: "'My God!' said the Czar, 'my plans are frustrated!'" It seemed an excellent occasion for being a black puma. Harold liked black pumas, on the whole, as well as any animal we were familiar with. So I launched myself on him, with the appropriate howl, rolling him over on the gravel.

Life may be said to be composed of things that come off and things that don't come off. This thing, unfortunately, was one of the things that didn't come off. From beneath me I heard a shrill cry of, "Oh, it's my sore knee!" And Harold wriggled himself free from the puma's clutches, bellowing dismally. Now, I honestly didn't know he had a sore knee, and, what's more, he knew I didn't know he had a sore knee. According to boy-ethics, therefore, his attitude was wrong, sore knee or not, and no apology was due from me. I made half-way advances, however, suggesting we should lie in ambush by the edge of the pond and cut off the ducks as they waddled down in simple, unsuspecting single file; then hunt them as bisons flying scattered over the vast prairie. A fascinating pursuit this, and strictly illicit. But Harold would none of my overtures, and retreated to the house wailing with full lungs.

Things were getting simply infernal. I struck out blindly for the open country; and even as I made for the gate a shrill voice from a window bade me keep off the flower-beds. When the gate had swung to behind me with a vicious click I felt better, and after ten minutes along the road it began to grow on me that some radical change was needed, that I was in a blind alley, and that this intolerable state of things must somehow cease. All that I could do I had already done. As well-meaning a fellow as ever stepped was pounding along the road that day, with an exceeding sore heart; one who only wished to live and let live, in touch with his fellows, and appreciating what joys life had to offer. What was wanted now was a complete change of environment. Somewhere in the world, I felt sure, justice and sympathy still resided. There were places called pampas, for instance, that sounded well. League upon league of grass, with just an occasional wild horse, and not a relation within the horizon! To a bruised spirit this seemed a sane and a healing sort of existence. There were other pleasant corners, again, where you dived for pearls and stabbed sharks in the stomach with your big knife. No relations would be likely to come interfering with you when thus blissfully occupied. And yet I did not wish—just yet— to have done with relations entirely. They should be made to feel their position first, to see themselves as they really were, and to wish—when it was too late—that they had behaved more properly.

Of all professions, the army seemed to lend itself the most thoroughly to the scheme. You enlisted, you followed the drum, you marched, fought, and ported arms, under strange skies, through unrecorded years. At last, at long last, your opportunity would come, when the horrors of war were flickering through the quiet country-side where you were cradled and bred, but where the memory of you had long been dim. Folk would run together, clamorous, palsied with fear; and among the terror- stricken groups would figure certain aunts. "What hope is left us?" they would ask themselves, "save in the clemency of the General, the mysterious, invincible General, of whom men tell such romantic tales?" And the army would march in, and the guns would rattle and leap along the village street, and, last of all, you—you, the General, the fabled hero—you would enter, on your coal-black charger, your pale set face seamed by an interesting sabre-cut. And then—but every boy has rehearsed this familiar piece a score of times. You are magnanimous, in fine—that goes without saying; you have a coal-black horse, and a sabre-cut, and you can afford to be very magnanimous. But all the same you give them a good talking-to.

This pleasant conceit simply ravished my soul for some twenty minutes, and then the old sense of injury began to well up afresh, and to call for new plasters and soothing syrups. This time I took refuge in happy thoughts of the sea. The sea was my real sphere, after all. On the sea, in especial, you could combine distinction with lawlessness, whereas the army seemed to be always weighted by a certain plodding submission to discipline. To be sure, by all accounts, the life was at first a rough one. But just then I wanted to suffer keenly; I wanted to be a poor devil of a cabin boy, kicked, beaten, and sworn at— for a time. Perhaps some hint, some inkling of my sufferings might reach their ears. In due course the sloop or felucca would turn up—it always did—the rakish-looking craft, black of hull, low in the water, and bristling with guns; the jolly Roger flapping overhead, and myself for sole commander. By and by, as usually happened, an East Indiaman would come sailing along full of relations—not a necessary relation would be missing. And the crew should walk the plank, and the captain should dance from his own yardarm, and then I would take the passengers in hand—that miserable group of well-known figures cowering on the quarterdeck!—and then—and then the same old performance: the air thick with magnanimity. In all the repertory of heroes, none is more truly magnanimous than your pirate chief.

When at last I brought myself back from the future to the actual present, I found that these delectable visions had helped me over a longer stretch of road than I had imagined; and I looked around and took my bearings. To the right of me was a long low building of grey stone, new, and yet not smugly so; new, and yet possessing distinction, marked with a character that did not depend on lichen or on crumbling semi-effacement of moulding and mullion. Strangers might have been puzzled to classify it; to me, an explorer from earliest years, the place was familiar enough. Most folk called it "The Settlement"; others, with quite sufficient conciseness for our neighbourhood, spoke of "them there fellows up by Halliday's"; others again, with a hint of derision, named them the "monks." This last title I supposed to be intended for satire, and knew to be fatuously wrong. I was thoroughly acquainted with monks—in books—and well knew the cut of their long frocks, their shaven polls, and their fascinating big dogs, with brandy-bottles round their necks, incessantly hauling happy travellers out of the snow. The only dog at the settlement was an Irish terrier, and the good fellows who owned him, and were owned by him, in common, wore clothes of the most nondescript order, and mostly cultivated side-whiskers. I had wandered up there one day, searching (as usual) for something I never found, and had been taken in by them and treated as friend and comrade. They had made me free of their ideal little rooms, full of books and pictures, and clean of the antimacassar taint; they had shown me their chapel, high, hushed, and faintly scented, beautiful with a strange new beauty born both of what it had and what it had not—that too familiar dowdiness of common places of worship. They had also fed me in their dining-hall, where a long table stood on trestles plain to view, and all the woodwork was natural, unpainted, healthily scrubbed, and redolent of the forest it came from. I brought away from that visit, and kept by me for many days, a sense of cleanness, of the freshness that pricks the senses—the freshness of cool spring water; and the large swept spaces of the rooms, the red tiles, and the oaken settles, suggested a comfort that had no connection with padded upholstery.

On this particular morning I was in much too unsociable a mind for paying friendly calls. Still, something in the aspect of the place harmonized with my humour, and I worked my way round to the back, where the ground, after affording level enough for a kitchen-garden, broke steeply away. Both the word Gothic and the thing itself were still unknown to me, yet doubtless the architecture of the place, consistent throughout, accounted for its sense of comradeship in my hour of disheartenment. As I mused there, with the low, grey, Purposeful-looking building before me, and thought of my pleasant friends within, and what good times they always seemed to be having, and how they larked with the Irish terrier, whose footing was one of a perfect equality, I thought of a certain look in their faces, as if they had a common purpose and a business, and were acting under orders thoroughly recognized and understood. I remembered, too, something that Martha had told me, about these same fellows doing "a power o' good," and other hints I had collected vaguely, of renouncements, rules, self-denials, and the like. Thereupon, out of the depths of my morbid soul swam up a new and fascinating idea; and at once the career of arms seemed over-acted and stale, and piracy, as a profession, flat and unprofitable. This, then, or something like it, should be my vocation and my revenge. A severer line of business, perhaps, such as I had read of; something that included black bread and a hair-shirt. There should be vows, too—irrevocable, blood-curdling vows; and an iron grating. This iron grating was the most necessary feature of all, for I intended that on the other side of it my relations should range themselves—I mentally ran over the catalogue, and saw that the whole gang was present, all in their proper places—a sad-eyed row, combined in tristful appeal. "We see our error now," they would say; "we were always dull dogs, slow to catch—especially in those akin to us—the finer qualities of soul! We misunderstood you, misappreciated you, and we own up to it. And now "Alas, my dear friends," I would strike in here, waving towards them an ascetic hand—one of the emaciated sort, that lets the light shine through at the fingertips—" Alas, you come too late! This conduct is fitting and meritorious on your part, and indeed I always expected it of you, sooner or later; but the die is cast, and you may go home again and bewail at your leisure this too tardy repentance of yours. For me, I am vowed and dedicated, and my relations henceforth are austerity and holy works. Once a month, should you wish it, it shall be your privilege to come and gaze at me through this very solid grating; but—" Whack! A well-aimed clod of garden soil, whizzing just past my ear, starred on a tree-trunk behind, spattering me with dirt, The present came back to me in a flash, and I nimbly took cover behind the trees, realizing that the enemy was up and abroad, with ambuscades, alarms, and thrilling sallies. It was the gardener's boy, I knew well enough; a red proletariat, who hated me just because I was a gentleman. Hastily picking up a nice sticky clod in one hand, with the other I delicately projected my hat beyond the shelter of the tree-trunk. I had not fought with Red-skins all these years for nothing. As I had expected, another clod, of the first class for size and stickiness, took my poor hat full in the centre. Then, Ajax-like, shouting terribly, I issued from shelter and discharged my ammunition. Woe then for the gardener's boy, who, unprepared, skipping in premature triumph, took the clod full in his stomach! He, the foolish one, witless on whose side the gods were fighting that day, discharged yet other missiles, wavering and wide of the mark; for his wind had been taken with the first clod, and he shot wildly, as one already desperate and in flight. I got another clod in at short range; we clinched on the brow of the hill, and rolled down to the bottom together. When he had shaken himself free and regained his legs, he trotted smartly off in the direction of his mother's cottage; but over his shoulder he discharged at me both imprecation and deprecation, menace mixed up with an under-current of tears.

But as for me, I made off smartly for the road, my frame tingling, my head high, with never a backward look at the Settlement of suggestive aspect, or at my well-planned future which lay in fragments around it. Life had its jollities, then; life was action, contest, victory! The present was rosy once more, surprises lurked on every side, and I was beginning to feel villainously hungry.

Just as I gained the road a cart came rattling by, and I rushed for it, caught the chain that hung below, and swung thrillingly between the dizzy wheels, choked and blinded with delicious- smelling dust, the world slipping by me like a streaky ribbon below, till the driver licked at me with his whip, and I had to descend to earth again. Abandoning the beaten track, I then struck homewards through the fields; not that the way was very much shorter, but rather because on that route one avoided the bridge, and had to splash through the stream and get refreshingly wet. Bridges were made for narrow folk, for people with aims and vocations which compelled abandonment of many of life's highest pleasures. Truly wise men called on each element alike to minister to their joy, and while the touch of sun-bathed air, the fragrance of garden soil, the ductible qualities of mud, and the spark-whirling rapture of playing with fire, had each their special charm, they did not overlook the bliss of getting their feet wet. As I came forth on the common Harold broke out of an adjoining copse and ran to meet me, the morning rain-clouds all blown away from his face. He had made a new squirrel-stick, it seemed. Made it all himself; melted the lead and everything! I examined the instrument critically, and pronounced it absolutely magnificent. As we passed in at our gate the girls were distantly visible, gardening with a zeal in cheerful contrast to their heartsick lassitude of the morning.

"There's bin another letter come to-day," Harold explained, "and the hamper got joggled about on the journey, and the presents worked down into the straw and all over the place. One of 'em turned up inside the cold duck. And that's why they weren't found at first. And Edward said, Thanks awfully!"

I did not see Martha again until we were all re-assembled at tea-time, when she seemed red-eyed and strangely silent, neither scolding nor finding fault with anything. Instead, she was very kind and thoughtful with jams and things, feverishly pressing unwonted delicacies on us, who wanted little pressing enough. Then suddenly, when I was busiest, she disappeared; and Charlotte whispered me presently that she had heard her go to her room and lock herself in. This struck me as a funny sort of proceeding.

The Magic Ring

Grown-up people really ought to be more careful. Among themselves it may seem but a small thing to give their word and take back their word. For them there are so many compensations. Life lies at their feet, a party-coloured india-rubber ball; they may kick it this way or kick it that, it turns up blue, yellow, or green, but always coloured and glistening. Thus one sees it happen almost every day, and, with a jest and a laugh, the thing is over, and the disappointed one turns to fresh pleasure, lying ready to his hand. But with those who are below them, whose little globe is swayed by them, who rush to build star-pointing alhambras on their most casual word, they really ought to be more careful.

In this case of the circus, for instance, it was not as if we had led up to the subject. It was they who began it entirely—prompted thereto by the local newspaper. "What, a circus!" said they, in their irritating, casual way: "that would be nice to take the children to. Wednesday would be a good day. Suppose we go on Wednesday. Oh, and pleats are being worn again, with rows of deep braid," etc.

What the others thought I know not; what they said, if they said anything, I did not comprehend. For me the house was bursting, walls seemed to cramp and to stifle, the roof was jumping and lifting. Escape was the imperative thing—to escape into the open air, to shake off bricks and mortar, and to wander in the unfrequented places of the earth, the more properly to take in the passion and the promise of the giddy situation.

Nature seemed prim and staid that day, and the globe gave no hint that it was flying round a circus ring of its own. Could they really be true, I wondered, all those bewildering things I had heard tell of circuses? Did long-tailed ponies really walk on their hind-legs and fire off pistols? Was it humanly possible for clowns to perform one-half of the bewitching drolleries recorded in history? And how, oh, how dare I venture to believe that, from off the backs of creamy Arab steeds, ladies of more than earthly beauty discharged themselves through paper hoops? No, it was not altogether possible, there must have been some exaggeration. Still, I would be content with very little, I would take a low percentage—a very small proportion of the circus myth would more than satisfy me.

But again, even supposing that history were, once in a way, no liar, could it be that I myself was really fated to look upon this thing in the flesh and to live through it, to survive the rapture? No, it was altogether too much. Something was bound to happen, one of us would develop measles, the world would blow up with a loud explosion. I must not dare, I must not presume, to entertain the smallest hope. I must endeavour sternly to think of something else.

Needless to say, I thought, I dreamed of nothing else, day or night. Waking, I walked arm-in-arm with a clown, and cracked a portentous whip to the brave music of a band. Sleeping, I pursued—perched astride of a coal-black horse—a princess all gauze and spangles, who always managed to keep just one unattainable length ahead. In the early morning Harold and I, once fully awake, cross-examined each other as to the possibilities of this or that circus tradition, and exhausted the lore long ere the first housemaid was stirring. In this state of exaltation we slipped onward to what promised to be a day of all white days—which brings me right back to my text, that grown-up people really ought to be more careful.

I had known it could never really be; I had said so to myself a dozen times. The vision was too sweetly ethereal for embodiment. Yet the pang of the disillusionment was none the less keen and sickening, and the pain was as that of a corporeal wound. It seemed strange and foreboding, when we entered the breakfast-room, not to find everybody cracking whips, jumping over chairs, and whooping in ecstatic rehearsal of the wild reality to come. The situation became grim and pallid indeed, when I caught the expressions "garden-party" and "my mauve tulle," and realised that they both referred to that very afternoon. And every minute, as I sat silent and listened, my heart sank lower and lower, descending relentlessly like a clock-weight into my boot soles.

Throughout my agony I never dreamed of resorting to a direct question, much less a reproach. Even during the period of joyful anticipation some fear of breaking the spell had kept me from any bald circus talk in the presence of them. But Harold, who was built in quite another way, so soon as he discerned the drift of their conversation and heard the knell of all his hopes, filled the room with wail and clamour of bereavement. The grinning welkin rang with "Circus!" "Circus!" shook the window-panes; the mocking walls re-echoed "Circus!" Circus he would have, and the whole circus, and nothing but the circus.

No compromise for him, no evasions, no fallacious, unsecured promises to pay. He had drawn his cheque on the Bank of Expectation, and it had got to be cashed then and there; else he would yell, and yell himself into a fit, and come out of it and yell again. Yelling should be his profession, his art, his mission, his career. He was qualified, he was resolute, and he was in no hurry to retire from the business.

The noisy ones of the world, if they do not always shout themselves into the imperial purple, are sure at least of receiving attention. If they cannot sell everything at their own price, one thing—silence—must, at any cost, be purchased of them. Harold accordingly had to be consoled by the employment of every specious fallacy and base-born trick known to those whose doom it is to handle children. For me their hollow cajolery had no interest, I could pluck no consolation out of their bankrupt though prodigal pledges. I only waited till that hateful, well-known "Some other time, dear!" told me that hope was finally dead. Then I left the room without any remark. It made it worse—if anything could—to hear that stale, worn-out old phrase, still supposed by those dullards to have some efficacy.

To nature, as usual, I drifted by instinct, and there, out of the track of humanity, under a friendly hedge-row had my black hour unseen. The world was a globe no longer, space was no more filled with whirling circuses of spheres. That day the old beliefs rose up and asserted themselves, and the earth was flat again—ditch-riddled, stagnant, and deadly flat. The undeviating roads crawled straight and white, elms dressed themselves stiffly along inflexible hedges, all nature, centrifugal no longer, sprawled flatly in lines out to its farthest edge, and I felt just like walking out to that terminus, and dropping quietly off. Then, as I sat there, morosely chewing bits of stick, the recollection came back to me of certain fascinating advertisements I had spelled out in the papers—advertisements of great and happy men, owning big ships of tonnage running into four figures, who yet craved, to the extent of public supplication, for the sympathetic co-operation of youths as apprentices. I did not rightly know what apprentices might be, nor whether I was yet big enough to be styled a youth, but one thing seemed clear, that, by some such means as this, whatever the intervening hardships, I could eventually visit all the circuses of the world—the circuses of merry France and gaudy Spain, of Holland and Bohemia, of China and Peru. Here was a plan worth thinking out in all its bearings; for something had presently to be done to end this intolerable state of things.

Mid-day, and even feeding-time, passed by gloomily enough, till a small disturbance occurred which had the effect of releasing some of the electricity with which the air was charged. Harold, it should be explained, was of a very different mental mould, and never brooded, moped, nor ate his heart out over any disappointment. One wild outburst—one dissolution of a minute into his original elements of air and water, of tears and outcry—so much insulted nature claimed. Then he would pull himself together, iron out his countenance with a smile, and adjust himself to the new condition of things.

If the gods are ever grateful to man for anything, it is when he is so good as to display a short memory. The Olympians were never slow to recognise this quality of Harold's, in which, indeed, their salvation lay, and on this occasion their gratitude had taken the practical form of a fine fat orange, tough-rinded as oranges of those days were wont to be. This he had eviscerated in the good old-fashioned manner, by biting out a hole in the shoulder, inserting a lump of sugar therein, and then working it cannily till the whole soul and body of the orange passed glorified through the sugar into his being. Thereupon, filled full of orange-juice and iniquity, he conceived a deadly snare. Having deftly patted and squeezed the orange-skin till it resumed its original shape, he filled it up with water, inserted a fresh lump of sugar in the orifice, and, issuing forth, blandly proffered it to me as I sat moodily in the doorway dreaming of strange wild circuses under tropic skies.

Such a stale old dodge as this would hardly have taken me in at ordinary moments. But Harold had reckoned rightly upon the disturbing effect of ill-humour, and had guessed, perhaps, that I thirsted for comfort and consolation, and would not criticise too closely the source from which they came. Unthinkingly I grasped the golden fraud, which collapsed at my touch, and squirted its contents into my eyes and over my collar, till the nethermost parts of me were damp with the water that had run down my neck. In an instant I had Harold down, and, with all the energy of which I was capable, devoted myself to grinding his head into the gravel; while he, realising that the closure was applied, and that the time for discussion or argument was past, sternly concentrated his powers on kicking me in the stomach.

Some people can never allow events to work themselves out quietly.

At this juncture one of Them swooped down on the scene, pouring shrill, misplaced abuse on both of us: on me for ill-treating my younger brother, whereas it was distinctly I who was the injured and the deceived; on him for the high offence of assault and battery on a clean collar—a collar which I had myself deflowered and defaced, shortly before, in sheer desperate ill-temper. Disgusted and defiant we fled in different directions, rejoining each other later in the kitchen-garden; and as we strolled along together, our short feud forgotten, Harold observed, gloomily: "I should like to be a cave-man, like Uncle George was tellin' us about: with a flint hatchet and no clothes, and live in a cave and not know anybody!"

"And if anyone came to see us we didn't like," I joined in, catching on to the points of the idea, "we'd hit him on the head with the hatchet till he dropped down dead."

"And then," said Harold, warming up, "we'd drag him into the cave and skin him!"

For a space we gloated silently over the fair scene our imaginations had conjured up. It was blood we felt the need of just then. We wanted no luxuries, nothing dear-bought nor far-fetched. Just plain blood, and nothing else, and plenty of it.

Blood, however, was not to be had. The time was out of joint, and we had been born too late. So we went off to the green-house, crawled into the heating arrangement underneath, and played at the dark and dirty and unrestricted life of cave-men till we were heartily sick of it. Then we emerged once more into historic times, and went off to the road to look for something living and sentient to throw stones at.

Nature, so often a cheerful ally, sometimes sulks and refuses to play. When in this mood she passes the word to her underlings, and all the little people of fur and feather take the hint and slip home quietly by back streets. In vain we scouted, lurked, crept, and ambuscaded. Everything that usually scurried, hopped, or fluttered—the small society of the undergrowth—seemed to have engagements elsewhere. The horrid thought that perhaps they had all gone off to the circus occurred to us simultaneously, and we humped ourselves up on the fence and felt bad. Even the sound of approaching wheels failed to stir any interest in us.

When you are bent on throwing stones at something, humanity seems obtrusive and better away. Then suddenly we both jumped off the fence together, our faces clearing. For our educated ear had told us that the approaching rattle could only proceed from a dog-cart, and we felt sure it must be the funny man.

We called him the funny man because he was sad and serious, and said little, but gazed right into our souls, and made us tell him just what was on our minds at the time, and then came out with some magnificently luminous suggestion that cleared every cloud away. What was more, he would then go off with us at once and play the thing right out to its finish, earnestly and devotedly, putting all other things aside. So we called him the funny man, meaning only that he was different from those others who thought it incumbent on them to play the painful mummer. The ideal as opposed to the real man was what we meant, only we were not acquainted with the phrase. Those others, with their laboured jests and clumsy contortions, doubtless flattered themselves that they were funny men; we, who had to sit through and applaud the painful performance, knew better.

He pulled up to a walk as soon as he caught sight of us, and the dog-cart crawled slowly along till it stopped just opposite. Then he leant his chin on his hand and regarded us long and soulfully, yet said he never a word; while we jigged up and down in the dust, grinning bashfully but with expectation. For you never knew exactly what this man might say or do.

"You look bored," he remarked presently; "thoroughly bored. Or else—let me see; you're not married, are you?"

He asked this in such sad earnestness that we hastened to assure him we were not married, though we felt he ought to have known that much; we had been intimate for some time.

"Then it's only boredom," he said. "Just satiety and world-weariness. Well, if you assure me you aren't married you can climb into this cart and I'll take you for a drive. I'm bored, too. I want to do something dark and dreadful and exciting."

We clambered in, of course, yapping with delight and treading all over his toes; and as we set off, Harold demanded of him imperiously whither he was going.

"My wife," he replied, "has ordered me to go and look up the curate and bring him home to tea. Does that sound sufficiently exciting for you?"

Our faces fell. The curate of the hour was not a success, from our point of view. He was not a funny man, in any sense of the word.

"—but I'm not going to," he added, cheerfully. "Then I was to stop at some cottage and ask—what was it? There was nettle-rash mixed up in it, I'm sure. But never mind, I've forgotten, and it doesn't matter. Look here, we're three desperate young fellows who stick at nothing. Suppose we go off to the circus?"

Of certain supreme moments it is not easy to write. The varying shades and currents of emotion may indeed be put into words by those specially skilled that way; they often are, at considerable length. But the sheer, crude article itself—the strong, live thing that leaps up inside you and swells and strangles you, the dizziness of revulsion that takes the breath like cold water—who shall depict this and live? All I knew was that I would have died then and there, cheerfully, for the funny man; that I longed for red

Indians to spring out from the hedge on the dog-cart, just to show what I would do; and that, with all this, I could not find the least little word to say to him.

Harold was less taciturn. With shrill voice, uplifted in solemn chant, he sang the great spheral circus-song, and the undying glory of the Ring. Of its timeless beginning he sang, of its fashioning by cosmic forces, and of its harmony with the stellar plan. Of horses he sang, of their strength, their swiftness, and their docility as to tricks. Of clowns again, of the glory of knavery, and of the eternal type that shall endure. Lastly he sang of Her—the Woman of the Ring—flawless, complete, untrammelled in each subtly curving limb; earth's highest output, time's noblest expression. At least, he doubtless sang all these things and more—he certainly seemed to; though all that was distinguishable was, "We're-goin'-to-the-circus!" and then, once more, "We're-goin'-to-the-circus!"—the sweet rhythmic phrase repeated again and again. But indeed I cannot be quite sure, for I heard confusedly, as in a dream. Wings of fire sprang from the old mare's shoulders. We whirled on our way through purple clouds, and earth and the rattle of wheels were far away below.

The dream and the dizziness were still in my head when I found myself, scarce conscious of intermediate steps, seated actually in the circus at last, and took in the first sniff of that intoxicating circus smell that will stay by me while this clay endures. The place was beset by a hum and a glitter and a mist; suspense brooded large o'er the blank, mysterious arena. Strung up to the highest pitch of expectation, we knew not from what quarter, in what divine shape, the first surprise would come.

A thud of unseen hoofs first set us a-quiver; then a crash of cymbals, a jangle of bells, a hoarse applauding roar, and Coralie was in the midst of us, whirling past 'twixt earth and sky, now erect, flushed, radiant, now crouched to the flowing mane; swung and tossed and moulded by the maddening dance-music of the band. The mighty whip of the count in the frock-coat marked time with pistol-shots; his war-cry, whooping clear above the music, fired the blood with a passion for splendid deeds, as Coralie, laughing, exultant, crashed through the paper hoops. We gripped the red cloth in front of us, and our souls sped round and round with Coralie, leaping with her, prone with her, swung by mane or tail with her. It was not only the ravishment of her delirious feats, nor her cream-coloured horse of fairy breed, long-tailed, roe-footed, an enchanted prince surely, if ever there was one! It was her more than mortal beauty—displayed, too, under conditions never vouchsafed to us before—that held us spell-bound. What princess had arms so dazzlingly white, or went delicately clothed in such pink and spangles? Hitherto we had known the outward woman as but a drab thing, hour-glass shaped, nearly legless, bunched here, constricted there, slow of movement, and given to deprecating lusty action of limb. Here was a revelation! From henceforth our imaginations would have to be revised and corrected up to date. In one of those swift rushes the mind makes in high-strung moments, I saw myself and Coralie, close enfolded, pacing the world together, o'er hill and plain, through storied cities, past rows of applauding relations,—I in my Sunday knickerbockers, she in her pink and spangles.

Summers sicken, flowers fail and die, all beauty but rides round the ring and out at the portal; even so Coralie passed in her turn, poised sideways, panting, on her steed; lightly swayed as a tulip-bloom, bowing on this side and on that as she disappeared; and with her went my heart and my soul, and all the light and the glory and the entrancement of the scene.

Harold woke up with a gasp. "Wasn't she beautiful?" he said, in quite a subdued way for him. I felt a momentary pang. We had been friendly rivals before, in many an exploit; but here was altogether a more serious affair. Was this, then, to be the beginning of strife and coldness, of civil war on the hearthstone and the sundering of old ties? Then I recollected the true position of things, and felt very sorry for Harold; for it was inexorably written that he would have to give way to me, since I was the elder. Rules were not made for nothing, in a sensibly constructed universe.

There was little more to wait for, now Coralie had gone; yet I lingered still, on the chance of her appearing again. Next moment the clown tripped up and fell flat, with magnificent artifice, and at once fresh emotions began to stir. Love had endured its little hour, and stern ambition now asserted itself. Oh, to be a splendid fellow like this, self-contained, ready of speech, agile beyond conception, braving the forces of society, his hand against everyone, yet always getting the best of it! What freshness of humour, what courtesy to dames, what triumphant ability to discomfit rivals, frock-coated and moustached though they might be! And what a grand, self-confident straddle of the legs! Who could desire a finer career than to go through life thus gorgeously equipped! Success was his keynote, adroitness his panoply, and the mellow music of laughter his instant reward. Even Coralie's image wavered and receded. I would come back to her in the evening, of course; but I would be a clown all the working hours of the day.

The short interval was ended: the band, with long-drawn chords, sounded a prelude touched with significance; and the programme, in letters overtopping their fellows, proclaimed Zephyrine, the Bride of the Desert, in her unequalled bareback equestrian interlude. So sated was I already with beauty and with wit, that I hardly dared hope for a fresh emotion. Yet her title was tinged with romance, and Coralie's display had aroused in me an interest in her sex which even herself had failed to satisfy entirely.

Brayed in by trumpets, Zephyrine swung passionately into the arena. With a bound she stood erect, one foot upon each of her supple, plunging Arabs, and at once I knew that my fate was sealed, my chapter closed, and the Bride of the Desert was the one bride for me. Black was her raiment, great silver stars shone through it, caught in the dusky twilight of her gauze; black as her own hair were the two mighty steeds she bestrode.

In a tempest they thundered by, in a whirlwind, a scirocco of tan; her cheeks bore the kiss of an Eastern sun, and the sand-storms of her native desert were her satellites. What was Coralie, with her pink silk, her golden hair and slender limbs, beside this magnificent, full-figured Cleopatra? In a twinkling we were scouring the desert—she and I and the two coal-black horses. Side by side, keeping pace in our swinging gallop, we distanced the ostrich, we outstrode the zebra; and, as we went, it seemed the wilderness blossomed like the rose.

I know not rightly how we got home that evening. On the road there were everywhere strange presences, and the thud of phantom hoofs encircled us. In my nose was the pungent circus-smell; the crack of the whip and the frank laugh of the clown were in my ears. The funny man thoughtfully abstained from conversation, and left our illusion quite alone, sparing us all jarring criticism and analysis; and he gave me no chance, when he deposited us at our gate, to get rid of the clumsy expressions of gratitude I had been laboriously framing. For the rest of the evening, distraught and silent, I only heard the march-music of the band, playing on in some corner of my brain. When at last my head touched the pillow, in a trice I was with Zephyrine, riding the boundless Sahara, cheek to cheek, the world well lost; while at times, through the sand-clouds that encircled us, glimmered the eyes of Coralie, touched, one fancied, with something of a tender reproach.

Mutabile Semper

She stood on the other side of the garden fence, and regarded me gravely as I came down the road. Then she said, "Hi—o!" and I responded, "Hullo!" and pulled up somewhat nervously.

To tell the truth, the encounter was not entirely unexpected on my part. The previous Sunday I had seen her in church, and after service it had transpired who she was, this new-comer, and what aunt she was staying with. That morning a volunteer had been called for, to take a note to the Parsonage, and rather to my own surprise I had found myself stepping forward with alacrity, while the others had become suddenly absorbed in various pursuits, or had sneaked unobtrusively out of view. Certainly I had not yet formed any deliberate plan of action; yet I suppose I recollected that the road to the Parsonage led past her aunt's garden.

She began the conversation, while I hopped backwards and forwards over the ditch, feigning a careless ease.

"Saw you in church on Sunday," she said; "only you looked different then. All dressed up, and your hair quite smooth, and brushed up at the sides, and oh, so shiny! What do they put on it to make it shine like that? Don't you hate having your hair brushed?" she ran on, without waiting for an answer. "How your boots squeaked when you came down the aisle! When mine squeak, I walk in all the puddles till they stop. Think I'll get over the fence."

This she proceeded to do in a businesslike way, while, with my hands deep in my pockets, I regarded her movements with silent interest, as those of some strange new animal.

"I've been gardening," she explained, when she had joined me, "but I didn't like it. There's so many worms about to-day. I hate worms. Wish they'd keep out of the way when I'm digging."

"Oh, I like worms when I'm digging," I replied heartily, "seem to make things more lively, don't they?"

She reflected. "Shouldn't mind 'em so much if they were warm and dry," she said, "but—" here she shivered, and somehow I liked her for it, though if it had been my own flesh and blood hoots of derision would have instantly assailed her,

From worms we passed, naturally enough, to frogs, and thence to pigs, aunts, gardeners, rocking-horses, and other fellow-citizens of our common kingdom. In five minutes we had each other's confidences, and I seemed to have known her for a lifetime. Somehow, on the subject of one's self it was easier to be frank and communicative with her than with one's female kin. It must be, I supposed, because she was less familiar with one's faulty, tattered past.

"I was watching you as you came along the road," she said presently, "and you had your head down and your hands in your pockets, and you weren't throwing stones at anything, or whistling, or jumping over things; and I thought perhaps you'd bin scolded, or got a stomachache."

"No," I answered shyly, "it wasn't that. Fact is, I was—I often—but it's a secret."

There I made an error in tactics. That enkindling word set her dancing round me, half beseeching, half imperious. "Oh, do tell it me!" she cried. "You must! I'll never tell anyone else at all, I vow and declare I won't!"

Her small frame wriggled with emotion, and with imploring eyes she jigged impatiently just in front of me. Her hair was tumbled bewitchingly on her shoulders, and even the loss of a front tooth—a loss incidental to her age—seemed but to add a piquancy to her face.

"You won't care to hear about it," I said, wavering. "Besides, I can't explain exactly. I think I won't tell you." But all the time I knew I should have to.

"But I do care," she wailed plaintively. "I didn't think you'd be so unkind!"

This would never do. That little downward tug at either corner of the mouth—I knew the symptom only too well!

"It 's like this," I began stammeringly. "This bit of road here—up as far as that corner—you know it 's a horrid dull bit of road. I'm always having to go up and down it, and I know it so well, and I'm so sick of it. So whenever I get to that corner, I just—well, I go right off to another place!"

"What sort of a place?" she asked, looking round her gravely.

"Of course it's just a place I imagine," I went on hurriedly and rather shamefacedly: "but it's an awfully nice place—the nicest place you ever saw. And I always go off there in church, or during joggraphy lessons."

"I'm sure it's not nicer than my home," she cried patriotically. "Oh, you ought to see my home—it 's lovely! We've got—"

"Yes it is, ever so much nicer," I interrupted. "I mean"—I went on apologetically—" of course I know your home's beautiful and all that. But this must be nicer, 'cos if you want anything at all, you've only got to want it, and you can have it!"

"That sounds jolly," she murmured. "Tell me more about it, please. Tell me how you get there, first."

"I—don't—quite—know—exactly," replied. "I just go. But generally it begins by—well, you're going up a broad, clear river in a sort of a boat. You're not rowing or anything—you're just moving along. And there's beautiful grass meadows on both sides, and the river's very full, quite up to the level of the grass. And you glide along by the edge. And the people are haymaking there, and playing games, and walking about; and they shout to you, and you shout back to them, and they bring you things to eat out of their baskets, and let you drink out of their bottles; and some of 'em are the nice people you read about in books. And so at last you come to the Palace steps—great broad marble steps, reaching right down to the water. And there at the steps you find every sort of boat you can imagine—schooners, and punts, and row-boats, and little men-of-war. And you have any sort of boating you want to—rowing, or sailing, or shoving about in a punt!"

"I'd go sailing," she said decidedly: "and I 'd steer. No, you'd have to steer, and I'd sit about on the deck. No, I wouldn't though; I'd row—at least I'd make you row, and I'd steer. And then we'd—Oh, no! I'll tell you what we do! We'd just sit in a punt and dabble!"

"Of course we'll do just what you like," I said hospitably; but already I was beginning to feel my liberty of action somewhat curtailed by this exigent visitor I had so rashly admitted into my sanctum.

I don't think we'd boat at all," she finally decided. "It's always so wobbly Where do you come to next?"

"You go up the steps," I continued, "and in at the door, and the very first place you come to is the Chocolate-room!"

She brightened up at this, and I heard her murmur with gusto, "Chocolate-room!"

"It's got every sort of chocolate you can think of," I went on: "soft chocolate, with sticky stuff inside, white and pink, what girls like; and hard shiny chocolate, that cracks when you bite it, and takes such a nice long time to suck!"

"I like the soft stuff best," she said: "'cos you can eat such a lot more of it!" This was to me a new aspect of the chocolate question, and I regarded her with interest and some respect. With us, chocolate was none too common a thing, and, whenever we happened to come by any, we resorted to the quaintest devices in order to make it last out. Still, legends had reached us of children who actually had, from time to time, as much chocolate as they could possibly eat; and here, apparently, was one of them.

"You can have all the creams," I said magnanimously, "and I'll eat the hard sticks, 'cos I like 'em best."

"Oh, but you mustn't!" she cried impetuously. "You must eat the same as I do! It isn't nice to want to eat different. I'll tell you what—you must give me all the chocolate, and then I'll give you—I'll give you what you ought to have!"

"Oh, all right," I said, in a subdued sort of way. It seemed a little hard to be put under a sentimental restriction like this in one s own Chocolate-room.

"In the next room you come to, "I proceeded, "there's fizzy drinks! There's a marble-slab business all round the room, and little silver taps; and you just turn the right tap, and have any kind of fizzy drink you want."

"What fizzy drinks are there?" she inquired.

"Oh, all sorts," I answered hastily, hurrying on. (She might restrict my eatables, but I'd be hanged if I was going to have her meddle with my drinks.) "Then you go down the corridor, and at the back of the palace there's a great big park—the finest park you ever saw. And there's ponies to ride on, and carriages and carts; and a little railway, all complete, engine and guard's van and all; and you work it yourself, and you can go first- class, or in the van, or on the engine, just whichever you choose."

"I'd go on the engine," she murmured dreamily. "No, I wouldn't, I'd—"

"Then there 's all the soldiers," I struck in. Really the line had to be drawn somewhere, and I could not have my railway system disorganized and turned upside down by a mere girl. "There's any quantity of 'em, fine big soldiers, and they all belong to me. And a row of brass cannons all along the terrace! And every now and then I give the order, and they fire off all the guns!"

"No, they don't," she interrupted hastily. "I won't have 'em fire off any guns You must tell 'em not to. I hate guns, and as soon as they begin firing I shall run right away!"

"But—but that 's what they're there for," I protested, aghast

"I don't care," she insisted. "They mustn't do it. They can walk about behind me if they like, and talk to me, and carry things. But they mustn't fire off any guns."

I was sadly conscious by this time that in this brave palace of mine, wherein I was wont to swagger daily, irresponsible and unquestioned, I was rapidly becoming—so to speak—a mere lodger. The idea of my fine big soldiers being told off to "carry things"! I was not inclined to tell her any more, though there still remained plenty more to tell.

"Any other boys there?" she asked presently, in a casual sort of way. "Oh yes," I unguardedly replied. "Nice chaps, too. We'll have great—" Then I recollected myself. "We'll play with them, of course," I went on. "But you are going to be my friend, aren't you? And you'll come in my boat, and we'll travel in the guard's van together, and I'll stop the soldiers firing off their guns!" But she looked mischievously away, and—do what I would—I could not get her to promise.

Just then the striking of the village clock awoke within me another clamorous timepiece, reminding me of mid-day mutton a good half-mile away, and of penalties and curtailments attaching to a late appearance. We took a hurried farewell of each other, and before we parted I got from her an admission that she might be gardening again that afternoon, if only the worms would be less aggressive and give her a chance.

"Remember," I said as I turned to go, "you mustn't tell anybody about what I've been telling you!"

She appeared to hesitate, swinging one leg to and fro while she regarded me sideways with half-shut eyes.

"It's a dead secret," I said artfully. "A secret between us two, and nobody knows it except ourselves!

Then she promised, nodding violently, big-eyed, her mouth pursed up small. The delight of revelation, and the bliss of possessing a secret, run each other very close. But the latter generally wins—for a time.

I had passed the mutton stage and was weltering in warm rice pudding, before I found leisure to pause and take in things generally; and then a glance in the direction of the window told me, to my dismay, that it was raining hard. This was annoying in every way, for, even if it cleared up later, the worms—I knew well from experience—would be offensively numerous and frisky. Sulkily I said grace and accompanied the others upstairs to the schoolroom; where I got out my paint-box and resolved to devote myself seriously to Art, which of late I had much neglected. Harold got hold of a sheet of paper and a pencil, retired to a table in the corner, squared his elbows, and protruded his tongue. Literature had always been his form of artistic expression.

Selina had a fit of the fidgets, bred of the unpromising weather, and, instead of settling down to something on her own account, must needs walk round and annoy us artists, intent on embodying our conceptions of the ideal. She had been looking over my shoulder some minutes before I knew of it; or I would have had a word or two to say upon the subject.

"I suppose you call that thing a ship," she remarked contemptuously. "Who ever heard of a pink ship? Hoo-hoo!"

I stifled my wrath, knowing that in order to score properly it was necessary to keep a cool head.

"There is a pink ship," I observed with forced calmness, "lying in the toyshop window now. You can go and look at it if you like. D' you suppose you know more about ships than the fellows who make 'em?"

Selina, baffled for the moment, returned to the charge presently.

"Those are funny things, too," she observed. "S'pose they 're meant to be trees. But they're blue."

"They are trees," I replied with severity; "and they are blue. They've got to be blue, 'cos you stole my gamboge last week, so I can't mix up any green."

"Didn't steal your gamboge," declared Selina, haughtily, edging away, however, in the direction of Harold. "And I wouldn't tell lies, either, if I was you, about a dirty little bit of gainboge."

I preserved a discreet silence. After all, I knew she knew she stole my gainboge.

The moment Harold became conscious of Selina's stealthy approach, he dropped his pencil and flung himself flat upon the table, protecting thus his literary efforts from chilling criticism by the interposed thickness of his person. From some- where in his interior proceeded a heart rending compound of squeal and whistle, as of escaping steam,—long-drawn, ear- piercing, unvarying in note.

"I only just wanted to see," protested Selina, struggling to uproot his small body from the scrawl it guarded. But Harold clung limpet-like to the table edge, and his shrill protest continued to deafen humanity and to threaten even the serenities of Olympus. The time seemed come for a demonstration in force. Personally I cared little what soul-outpourings of Harold were priated by Selina—she was pretty sure to get hold of them sooner or later—and indeed I rather welcomed the diversion as favourable to the undisturbed pursuit of Art. But the clannishness of sex has its unwritten laws. Boys, as such, are sufficiently put upon, maltreated, trodden under, as it is. Should they fail to hang together in perilous times, what disasters, what ignominies may not be looked for? Possibly even an extinction of the tribe. I dropped my paint brush and sailed shouting into the fray.

The result for a short space hung dubious. There is a period of life when the difference of a year or two in age far outweighs the minor advantage of sex. Then the gathers of Selina's frock came away with a sound like the rattle of distant musketry; and this calamity it was, rather than mere brute compulsion, that quelled her indomitable spirit.

The female tongue is mightier than the sword, as I soon had good reason to know, when Selina, her riven garment held out at length, avenged her discomfiture with the Greek-fire of personalities and abuse. Every black incident in my short, but not stainless, career—every error, every folly, every penalty ignobly suffered—were paraded before me as in a magic-lantern show. The information, however, was not particularly new to me, and the effect was staled by previous rehearsals. Besides, a victory remains a victory, whatever the moral character of the triumphant general.

Harold chuckled and crowed as he dropped from the table, revealing the document over which so many gathers had sighed their short lives out. "You can read it if you like," he said to me gratefully. "It's only a Death-letter."

It had never been possible to say what Harold's particular amusement of the hour might turn out to be. One thing only was certain, that it would be something improbable, unguessable, not to be foretold. Who, for instance, in search of relaxation, would ever dream of choosing the drawing-up of a testamentary disposition of property? Yet this was the form taken by Harold's latest craze; and in justice this much had to be said for him, that in the christening of his amusement he had gone right to the heart of the matter. The words "will" and "testament" have various meanings and uses; but about the signification of "death- letter" there can be no manner of doubt. I smoothed out the crumpled paper and read. In actual form it deviated considerably from that usually adopted by family solicitors of standing, the only resemblance, indeed, lying in the absence of punctuation.

"my dear edward (it ran) when I die I leave all my muny to you my walkin sticks wips my crop my sord and gun bricks forts and all things i have goodbye my dear charlotte when die I leave you my wach and cumpus and pencel case my salors and camperdown my picteres and evthing goodbye your loving brother armen my dear Martha I love you very much i leave you my garden my mice and rabets my plants in pots when I die please take care of them my dear—" Catera desunt.

"Why, you 're not leaving me anything!" exclaimed Selina, indignantly. "You're a regular mean little boy, and I'll take back the last birthday present I gave you!"

"I don't care," said Harold, repossessing himself of the document. "I was going to leave you something, but I sha'n't now, 'cos you tried to read my death-letter before I was dead!"

"Then I'll write a death-letter myself," retorted Selina, scenting an artistic vengeance: "and I sha'n't leave you a single thing!" And she went off in search of a pencil.

The tempest within-doors had kept my attention off the condition of things without. But now a glance through the window told me that the rain had entirely ceased, and that everything was bathed instead in a radiant glow of sunlight, more golden than any gamboge of mine could possibly depict. Leaving Selina and Harold to settle their feud by a mutual disinheritance, I slipped from the room and escaped into the open air, eager to pick up the loose end of my new friendship just where I had dropped it that morning. In the glorious reaction of the sunshine after the downpour, with its moist warm smells, bespanglement of greenery, and inspiriting touch of rain-washed air, the parks and palaces of the imagination glowed with a livelier iris, and their blurred beauties shone out again with fresh blush and palpitation. As I sped along to the tryst, again I accompanied my new comrade along the corridors of my pet palace into which I had so hastily introduced her; and on reflection I began to see that it wouldn't work properly. I had made a mistake, and those were not the surroundings in which she was most fitted to shine. However, it really did not matter much; I had other palaces to place at her disposal—plenty of 'em; and on a further acquaintance with and knowledge of her tastes, no doubt I could find something to suit her.

There was a real Arabian one, for instance, which I visited but rarely—only just when I was in the fine Oriental mood for it; a wonder of silk hangings, fountains of rosewater, pavilions, and minarets. Hundreds of silent, well-trained slaves thronged the stairs and alleys of this establishment, ready to fetch and carry for her all day, if she wished it; and my brave soldiers would be spared the indignity. Also there were processions through the bazaar at odd moments—processions with camels, elephants, and palanquins. Yes, she was more suited for the East, this imperious young person; and I determined that thither she should be personally conducted as soon as ever might be.

I reached the fence and climbed up two bars of it, and leaning over I looked this way and that for my twin-souled partner of the morning. It was not long before I caught sight of her, only a short distance away. Her back was towards me and—well, one can never foresee exactly how one will find things—she was talking to a Boy.

Of course there are boys and boys, and Lord knows I was never narrow. But this was the parson's son from an adjoining village, a red-headed boy and as common a little beast as ever stepped. He cultivated ferrets—his only good point; and it was evidently through the medium of this art that he was basely supplanting me, for her head was bent absorbedly over something he carried in his hands. With some trepidation I called out, "Hi!" But answer there was none. Then again I called, "Hi!" but this time with a sickening sense of failure and of doom. She replied only by a complex gesture, decisive in import if not easily described. A petulant toss of the head, a jerk of the left shoulder, and a backward kick of the left foot, all delivered at once—that was all, and that was enough. The red-headed boy never even condescended to glance my way. Why, indeed, should he? I dropped from the fence without another effort, and took my way homewards along the weary road.

Little inclination was left to me, at first, for any solitary visit to my accustomed palace, the pleasures of which I had so recently tasted in company; and yet after a minute or two I found myself, from habit, sneaking off there much as usual. Presently I became aware of a certain solace and consolation in my newly- recovered independence of action. Quit of all female whims and fanciful restrictions, I rowed, sailed, or punted, just as I pleased; in the Chocolate-room I cracked and nibbled the hard sticks, with a certain contempt for those who preferred the soft, veneered article; and I mixed and quaffed countless fizzy drinks without dread of any prohibitionist. Finally, I swaggered into the park, paraded all my soldiers on the terrace, and, bidding them take the time from me, gave the order to fire off all the guns.

The Iniquity of Oblivion

Aman I know is fond of asking the irritating question—and in putting it he regards neither age nor sex, neither ancient friendship nor the rawest nodding acquaintance—"Did you ever forget an invitation to dinner?"

Of course the denial is prompt, passionate, and invariable. There are few crimes of which one would not rather be accused than this. He who cannot summon up the faintest blush at the recollection of having once said "Season," when no money had passed between him and the Railway Company whose guest he was for the moment—of having under-stated his income for purposes of taxation—or of having told his wife he was going to church, and then furtively picked up a fishing-rod as he passed through the hall—will colour angrily at the most innocent suggestion of a single possible lapse of memory regarding an invitation to dinner. But, none the less, every one finds it a little difficult to meet the natural rejoinder: "How do you know?"

Indeed, no other reply but painful silence is possible. To say, "Because I do," is natural enough, and frequently quite conclusive of further argument; still, it can hardly be called a reasoned refutation. The fact is, you don't know, and you cannot know. Your conviction that you do is based, first, on some sort of idea that you are bound to recollect, sooner or later, anything that you may have forgotten: an argument that only requires to be stated to display its fallacy; secondly, on a vague belief that a defection of so flagrant a character must inevitably be brought home to you by an incensed host or hostess—a theory that makes no allowance for the blissful sense of injury and offended pride, the joy of brooding over a wrong, which is one of the chief pleasures left to humanity. No: one doesn't know, and one can't know: and the past career of the most self-satisfied of us is doubtless littered with the debris of forgotten invitations.

Of course invitations, being but a small part of life, and not—as some would imply by their practice—its chief end, must be taken to stand here for much besides. One has only to think of the appalling amount of book-lore one has "crammed" in days gone by, and of the pitiful fragments that survive, to realise that facts, deeds, achievements, experiences numberless, may just as well have been hurried along the dusty track to oblivion. And once it has been fairly brought home to us that we have entirely forgotten any one thing—why, the gate is open. It is clear we may just as easily have forgotten hundreds.

This lamentable position of things was specially forced upon me, some time ago, by a certain persistent dream that used to wing its way to my bedside, not once or twice, but coming a dozen times, and always (I felt sure at the time) from out the Ivory Portal. First, there would be a sense of snugness, of cushioned comfort, of home-coming. Next, a gradual awakening to consciousness in a certain little room, very dear and familiar, sequestered in some corner of the more populous and roaring part of London: solitary, the world walled out, but full of a brooding sense of peace and of possession. At times I would make my way there, unerringly, through the wet and windy streets, climb the well-known staircase, open the ever-welcoming door. More often I was there already, ensconced in the most comfortable chair in the world, the lamp lit, the fire glowing ruddily. But always the same feeling of a home-coming, of the world shut out, of the ideal encasement. On the shelves were a few books—a very few—but just the editions I had sighed for, the editions which refuse to turn up, or which poverty glowers at on alien shelves. On the walls were a print or two, a woodcut, an etching—not many. Old loves, all of them, apparitions that had flashed across the field of view in sale-rooms and vanished again in a blaze of three figures; but never possessed—until now. All was modest—O, so very modest! But all was my very own, and, what was more, everything in that room was exactly right.

After three or four visits, the uncanniness of the repetition set me thinking. Could it possibly be, that this was no dream at all? Had this chamber, perhaps, a real existence, and was I all the time leading, somewhere, another life—a life within a life—a life that I constantly forgot, within the life that I happened to remember? I tried my best to bring the thing to absolute proof. First, there was that frequent sense of extreme physical weariness with which I was wont to confront the inevitable up-rising of the morning—might not that afford a clue? Alas, no: I traced my mornings back, far behind the beginnings of the dream. I could not remember a day, since those rare white ones at school when it was a whole holiday, and summer was boon and young, when I had faced the problem of getting up with anything but a full sense of disgust. Next I thought, I will consult my accounts. Rooms must be paid for in London, however modest they may be; and the blessed figures can't lie. Then I recollected that I did not keep any accounts—never had kept any accounts—never intended to keep any beastly accounts—and, on the whole, I confess I was rather glad. Statistics would have been a mean prosaic way of plucking out the heart of this mystery. My only chance seemed to lie in coming across the place by accident. Then perhaps the extinguished torch would re-kindle, the darkened garret of memory would be re-illumed, and it would be in my power at last to handle those rare editions, not capriciously as now, but at any hour I pleased. So I haunted Gray's Inn, Staple Inn, Clifford's Inn; hung about by-streets in Bloomsbury, even backwaters in Chelsea; but all to no result. It waits, that sequestered chamber, it waits for the serene moment when the brain is in just the apt condition, and ready to switch on the other memory even as one switches on the electric light with a turn of the wrist. Fantasy? well—perhaps. But the worst of it is, one never can feel quite sure. Only a dream, of course. And yet—the enchanting possibility!

And this possibility, which (one feels convinced) the wilful brain could make reality in a moment if it were only in the right humour, might be easily brought about by some accidental physical cause, some touch, scent, sound, gifted with the magic power of recall. Could my fingers but pass over the smooth surface of those oak balustrades so familiar to me, in a trice I would stand at the enchanted door. Could I even see in some casual shop-window one of those prints my other existence hoards so safe and sure—but that is unlikely indeed. Those prints of the dim land of dreams, "they never are sold in the merchant's mart!" Still, if one were only to turn up, in twopenny box or dusty portfolio, down in Southwark, off the roaring Strand, or somewhere along the quaint unclassified Brompton Road, in a flash the darkness would be day, the crooked would be made straight, and no policeman would be called upon to point out the joyous way.

If I have special faith in this sort of divining-rod, it is because of a certain strange case I once encountered and never quite elucidated. There was a certain man, respectable enough in every particular; wore drab spars all the year round, lived in a suburb, and did daily business on the "Baltic." When the weather was fine, and a halcyon calm brooded o'er the surface of the Baltic, instead of taking his suburban train at Cannon Street, he used to walk as far as Charing Cross: and before departing, if time allowed, he would turn into the National Gallery. Of a catholic mind, for he had never strayed down the tortuous byways of Art, he only went in to be amused, and was prepared to take his entertainment from all schools alike, without any of the narrow preferences of the cultured. From the very first, however, the Early Tuscans gripped him with a strange fascination, so that he rarely penetrated any further. What it was precisely that so detained him could never be ascertained. The man was not apt in the expression of subtle emotion, and never succeeded in defining the strong "possession"—for such it seemed to be—by which he was caught and held. The next phase in the case was, that he took to disappearing. He disappeared literally and absolutely—sometimes for a few days, sometimes for a fortnight or more; and on his return could tell nothing, explain nothing. Indeed, he did not seem to be really conscious of any absence. It was noted in time that his disappearances always coincided with his visits to the National Gallery. Thither he could be tracked; there all trace of him would cease. His female relations—an unimaginative, uneducated crew—surmised the unkindest things in their narrow way. Still, even they found it difficult to fling a stone at the Early Tuscans. For myself, I like to think that there was some bit of another life hidden away in him—some tranced memory of another far-away existence on Apennine slopes —which some quality in these pictures, and in these alone, had power to evoke. And I love to think that, transformed by this magic touch back into the other man of him, he passed, dream-possessed, forth from the portico, through Trafalgar Square, and into Charing Cross Station. That there, oblivious of all suburbs, he purchased one of those little books of coupons so much more romantic than your vulgar inland slip of pasteboard, and in due course sped Southwards—irresistibly drawn,—took the Alps in a series of whorls, burrowings, and breathless flights o'er torrent and fall—till he basked at last, still speeding South, in the full sunlight that steeps the Lombard plain. Arrived in time, where his destiny (which was also his past) awaited him, I could see him, avoiding clamour of piazza, shunning prim airlessness of Galleria and Accademia, climbing the white road to where, in some little village or red-tiled convent, lurked the creation, madonna or saint, that held the other end of the subtle thread. The boy-lover, had he been, of this prim-tressed model? Or the St. George or homely St. Roch who guarded her? Or himself the very painter? Whatever the bond, here I could imagine him to linger, steeping his soul in the picture and in the surroundings so native both to it and to the man whose life for a brief minute he lived again, till such time as that sullen devil within him—the later memory of the man he also was—began to stir drowsily and to urge him homewards, even as the other had urged him out. Once back, old sights and sounds would develop the later man into full being and consciousness, and as before he would tread the floor of the Baltic, while oblivion swallowed the Tuscan existence—until the next time!

These instances, it is true, are but "sports" in oblivion-lore, But, putting aside such puzzle-fragments of memory, it is impossible not to realise, in sad seriousness, that of all our recollection has once held, by far the larger part must be by this time in the realm of the forgot; and that every day some fresh delightful little entity pales, sickens, and passes over to the majority. Sir Thomas Browne has quaintly written concerning the first days of the young world, "when the living might exceed the dead, and to depart this World could not be properly said, to go unto the greater number"; but in these days of crowded thought, of the mind cultured and sensitised to receive such a swarm of impressions, no memory that sighs its life out but joins a host far exceeding what it leaves behind. 'Tis but a scanty wallet that each of us carries at his back. Few, indeed, and of a sorry mintage, the thin coins that jingle therein. Our gold, lightly won, has been as lightly scattered, along waysides left far behind. Oblivion, slowly but surely stalking us, gathers it with a full arm, and on the floor of his vast treasure-house stacks it in shining piles.

And if it is the larger part that has passed from us, why not also the better part? Indeed, logic almost requires it; for to select and eliminate, to hold fast and let go at will, is not given to us. As we jog along life's highroad, the knowledge of this inability dogs each conscious enjoyment, till with every pleasant experience comes also the annoying reflection, that it is a sheer toss-up whether this is going to be a gain, a solid profit to carry along with us, or fairy gold that shall turn to dust and nothingness in a few short mornings at best. As we realise our helplessness in the matter, we are almost ready to stamp and to swear. Will no one discover the chemical which shall fix the fleeting hue? That other recollection, now—that humiliating, that disgusting experience of ten years ago—that is safe enough, permanent, indestructible, warranted not to fade. If in this rag-fair we were only allowed to exchange and barter, to pick and choose! Oblivion, looking on, smiles grimly. It is he that shall select, not we; our part is but to look on helplessly, while—though he may condescend to leave us a pearl or two—the bulk of our jewels is swept into his pocket.

One hope alone remains to us, by way of consolation. These memories whose passing we lament, they are torpid only, not dead. They lie in a charmed sleep, whence a chance may awaken them, a touch make the dry bones live; though at present we know not the waking spell. Like Arthur, they have not perished, but only passed, and like him they may come again from the Avalon where they slumber. The chance is small, indeed. But the Merlin who controls these particular brain-cells, fitful and capricious though he be, after the manner of magicians, has powers to which we dare not assign limits. At any moment the stop may be pulled out, the switch pressed, the key turned, the Princess kissed. Then shall the spell-bound spring to life, the floodgates rise, the baked arid canals gleam with the silver tide; and once more we shall be fulfilled of the old joys, the old thrills, the old tears and laughter.

Better still—perhaps best of all—as those joyous old memories, hale and fresh once more, troop out of the catacombs into the light, these insistent ones of the present, this sullen host that beleaguers us day and night with such threatening obsession, may vanish, may pass, may flee away utterly, gone in their turn to lodge with Oblivion!—and a good riddance!

Printed in Great Britain
by Amazon